MY BEST FRIEND
MEE-YUNG KIM

Other *Best Friend* Books

My Best Friend, Duc Tran
Meeting a Vietnamese-American Family
by Dianne MacMillan and Dorothy Freeman

My Best Friend, Elena Pappas
Meeting a Greek-American Family
by Phyllis S. Yingling

My Best Friend, Martha Rodriguez
Meeting a Mexican-American Family
by Dianne MacMillan and Dorothy Freeman

My Best Friend, Tony Santos
Meeting a Portuguese-American Family
by Phyllis S. Yingling

MY BEST FRIEND MEE-YUNG KIM

Meeting a Korean-American Family

DIANNE MACMILLAN AND
DOROTHY FREEMAN

Pictures by Bob Marstall

Julian Messner

JULIAN MESSNER and colophon are
trademarks of Simon & Schuster, Inc.

Design by Meredith Dunham

Manufactured in the United States of America.

10 9 8 7 6 5 4 3 2 1

Library of Congress Cataloging-in-Publication Data

MacMillan, Dianne.
    My best friend, Mee-Yung Kim: meeting a Korean-American family/
Dianne MacMillan and Dorothy Freeman; pictures by Bob Marstall.
    p. cm.
    Bibliography: p. 39
    Summary: A young girl's friendship with a Korean-American girl and
her family introduces her to the holidays, customs, and foods and
family events of their culture.
    [1. Korean Americans—Social life and customs—Fiction. 2. Family
life—Fiction. 3. Friendship—Fiction.] I. Freeman, Dorothy
Rhodes. II. Marstall, Bob. III. Title.
PZ7.M2279Mym 1989
[Fic]—dc20   89-3274
                                                                   CIP
                                                                   AC
        ISBN 0-671-65691-0 (lib. bdg.)

Contents

Acknowledgements

The authors would like to thank their Korean-American friends for their assistance, and especially Dr. Chong K. Park, California State Department of Education, Bilingual Education Office; and Mr. Howard Kwan, ABC Unified School District, Cerritos, California.

1

The Harvest Festival Parade

Mee-Yung Kim and I sat next to each other in social studies. I didn't know her very well until the "Salad Bowl" project. That was when we became best friends.

"There are people from many countries in this class," Mr. Clark, our teacher, said. "That's one of the good things about living in Los Angeles. We're a mixture like a salad in a bowl!" Then he gave us an assignment. "If your parents were born in this country, choose a partner whose parents came from another country. Try to find out about customs that are different from those of other Americans. Are the same holidays celebrated? How are things done at home? Later you'll report to the class on what you learn from each other."

I turned to ask Mee-Yung Kim to be my partner because she's Korean-American. "Want to work together?" I asked.

"Sure, Bonnie, I was just going to ask you," she said. We decided to report on Mee-Yung's family.

Mee-Yung is really an American. She was born in the United States, but her parents were born in Korea. She says that her family has some Korean ways and some American ways.

Her father's a doctor. Most of his patients are Korean, so he speaks Korean to them. Her mother works in a bank and speaks English there.

At afternoon recess Mee-Yung said, "There's a Korean Harvest Festival parade next Saturday. You could see a lot of Korean customs there."

"I'd love to go to it!" I said.

"Great! You'll like the floats! My sister Alina and I are riding on one," she said.

I got up early on Saturday. I was excited about the festival. I took my camera to take pictures for our report.

At Mee-Yung's house, she and her sister came out to meet me. They were wearing long, beautiful dresses. Mee-Yung's was white on top and had a pink skirt with gold trimming.

She whirled to show the dress. Then she smiled at her sister and said to me, "This is Alina. She's in seventh grade." Alina's dress was all white with blue and gold borders on the sleeves and skirt. I was glad I had my camera to take their picture.

Alina said, "Korean clothes are called *hanbok*."

A tall, pretty woman came out of the house and Mee-Yung introduced her mother, Mrs. Chung. I wondered why she wasn't called Mrs. Kim, but I didn't ask.

Mee-Yung said, "The parade's going to be in Koreatown. That's the Korean business section of Los Angeles. My father's office is there."

When we got to Koreatown, I couldn't read the signs. Mee-Yung said they were in Chinese and Korean. At the place where the parade was starting, there were hundreds of girls and boys in bright colored *hanbok,* Korean clothing. I recognized Chi-Won Lee, a boy from our class. He was wearing a white shirt, baggy white pants, and a green belt. "Hi!" he said to Mee-Yung. "Which float are you riding on?"

"The Korean Chamber of Commerce float," Alina said. Then she looked at me and added, "That's an honor because they're in charge of the festival."

"That's my *Tae Kwon Do* class." Chi-Won pointed to a group of boys that were lining up to be in the parade. "Wait until you see what we're going to do! Watch for me in the parade."

We went to the place where the floats were waiting. Mee-Yung and Alina climbed on the Korean Chamber of Commerce float. Mrs. Chung helped them spread their skirts. They practiced waving to the crowd.

I sat on the curb and looked around at all the Korean stores. Behind me was a furniture store. In the store window were shiny black tables and chests.

The floats were decorated with plastic flower petals. Mee-Yung's float had one huge flower with heart-

3

shaped petals. Mee-Yung and Alina and other Korean girls sat by the petals.

After a while Mee-Yung's mother sat on the curb with me. When the floats started to move, we stood up to get a better view. Most of the people on the floats were children. Some were very little, but they smiled and waved.

On the front of the Korean Air Lines' float, a large orange-and-black tiger looked like he was waving his paw. "He's *Hodori,* the Korean mascot for the 1988 Seoul Olympics," Mrs. Chung said.

Another float had a white grand piano on it. All the children riding on this float were dressed in white and the flower petals were white and silver.

"That's Mee-Yung's music teacher playing the piano," Mrs. Chung said.

"I've never seen a piano in a parade before," I said.

"Almost all Korean children take music lessons. Music is really important to us," she said.

Suddenly there was the beat of drums as a group of boys marched by. Each boy had a red drum shaped like an hourglass. The drums were large and I thought they must be heavy. They were held by red cloth straps that went around the boys' necks and bodies. As we watched, the boys beat both sides of the drums with sticks.

"The drums are called *changgo,*" Mrs. Chung said. "Sometimes they are beaten with the hands instead of sticks."

"Do you have a *changgo* at home?" I asked.

"Yes, we have several, and Mee-Yung can bring one to school for the report."

I heard loud shouts and saw the boys from Chi-Won's class. They were marching and Chi-Won was in the first row. The parade stopped. Some of the boys got into a formation that looked like they were going to do gymnastics. One held a square piece of wood above his head. Another stood with his head bowed. Chi-Won knelt on the ground with his head tucked under and his back held high. Suddenly a boy ran, jumped onto Chi-Won's back, then onto the shoulders of the other boy. He hurled himself into the air, feet first. He shouted "Hiyuh" and kicked the board held by the third boy. It split and fell to the ground.

The jumper landed on his feet and bowed. Chi-Won and the other boys bowed, too. Everyone watching them cheered and clapped.

"Is that karate?" I asked.

"It's like karate, but it's called *Tae Kwon Do*," Mrs. Chung said.

There were more floats and high school bands and decorated cars. A man with a pushcart was selling Korean and American flags. I bought a Korean flag to take to school. I asked Mrs. Chung the meaning of the design in the center of the flag.

"The blue and red design in the circle is an ancient symbol of the universe. It stands for balance and harmony and also for opposites, like day and night, heat and cold."

There were sets of black bars in the corners of the flag. I asked what they meant.

"They're also ancient symbols. They stand for heaven, earth, fire, and water," Mrs. Chung explained. "Most Korean families have Korean and American flags. We're proud of both countries." I began to see what Mee-Yung meant when she said we'd get a lot of ideas for our report from the Harvest Festival.

A group of eight girls stopped in front of us. I looked at their bright red *hanbok* and the pink and green fans they carried. As music came from a loudspeaker on a float behind them, they waved their fans and danced.

After they moved on, a masked dancer began to perform. He was dressed in a blue vest and white pants.

"Watch when the dancer turns," Mrs. Chung said.

In a few seconds the dancer whirled around. From this view the dancer was a woman, with a woman's mask and a green blouse and red skirt.

Mrs. Chung saw my surprised look and said, "This is called the Mask Dance. The dancer's mask shows both man and woman—the two sides of human nature."

"Where do they learn to do the dances?" I asked.

"In the *Kugak* Society, a group that preserves the traditional music and dances of Korea. The dances you just saw have been performed for thousands of years."

It was hard for me to imagine anything being that old.

After the last float passed, we went to the park. Mrs. Chung went to meet Mee-Yung and Alina. There were stands selling Korean food. I bought something that looked like a pancake. The old man making the pancakes pointed to a red sauce and asked if I wanted some. I said I'd try it. When I took a bite of the pancake, I felt like my mouth was on fire. I fanned it with my hand.

Mee-Yung and Alina and their mother found me. Mrs. Chung laughed when I told her about the hot sauce. "Red peppers!" she said. "Why don't you come over to our house for dinner on Monday? I'll fix you some Korean food you'll like." She bought us all some cold punch. That cooled my mouth.

2

Treasures in Mee-Yung's Home

When we got back to Mee-Yung's house, she asked me to come in. She opened the door and took off her shoes. She put them in a row with other shoes. Then she put on a pair of slippers. I started to take my shoes off, but she shook her head. "You don't have to do that," she said. "We do it as a custom, and because it keeps the carpets cleaner."

"I'd like to do it the Korean way," I said. She gave me a pair of slippers to wear.

After she changed clothes Mee-Yung showed me her *hanbok.* "It's really a skirt and blouse. It doesn't have any zippers or buttons. The blouse is called *chogori* and the skirt's a *chima.*" She showed me how the bottom of the blouse had a tie that went around her waist and made a bow in front. "My mother said I can wear it when we give our report."

Alina came in with her *hanbok* over her arm. "Bonnie, you can wear mine when you give the report," she said. "I'm taller than you are, but you can wear the skirt higher."

"Oh, thank you! I'll take good care of it."

Alina said, "Our grandmother brought them back on her last visit to Korea, but you can buy them here."

"When do you wear them?" I asked.

"On special occasions, like birthdays and New Year's Day," Mee-Yung said.

"Why New Year's?"

"New Year's Day is when we give honor to our ancestors and our grandparents and parents. I'll tell you about it later. Come on, I want to show you some other things."

In the front hall she pointed to a large, pale green vase. It was covered with a design of circles and birds.

"It's beautiful," I whispered.

"It's called *celadon* ware. The birds are cranes and they're a symbol of long life. My father says that Korean people have been making vases like this for over a thousand years. He collects Korean pottery and this is his best piece. It's too valuable to bring to school, but you can take a picture of it."

I followed Mee-Yung into their living room. "This is a crown made for a king who wore it more than a thousand years ago." Mee-Yung stood in front of a golden crown in a glass case. I wondered how a king wore it because it was much too small to fit on a person's head.

"How did you get a king's crown? And why is it so small?" I asked.

"Oh, it's a miniature copy. The real one is in a museum in Korea."

"Did this one come from Korea?" I asked.

"No, from a store in the Korean shopping center. It was a birthday present to Alina from our father."

"What's that?" I asked, pointing to a long cord on the wall. There were three embroidered circles on the cord and the center one was the largest. The design on it was a peacock with his tail spread. There were tassels on the end of the cord.

"It's a wall decoration, but I have a small one to wear. I'll show you." Mee-Yung went to her room and came back with a small round piece of jewelry. It had many colors and two tassels. "Sometimes I wear this on the bow of my *hanbok.*" She opened the round part and explained that ladies used to put perfume inside. "That's why it's called a *perfume case,*" she said.

I was going to take a picture of it, but Mee-Yung said she could bring the perfume case to school.

I thanked Mee-Yung and Mrs. Chung for taking me to the festival.

Mee-Yung walked out with me as I left. I asked her about her mother's name. "Chung was her family name before she married. Most Korean women keep their own names," Mee-Yung explained.

"Could I ask you about your name?" I asked.

"Sure, what do you want to know?"

"Well, how come you have a Korean name and your sister doesn't?"

"Most of the Korean kids born here have American names. My brother's name is Peter. But I was named after my aunt, Mee-Yung. Our name means 'Beautiful Glory.'"

"That's a wonderful name, and I loved all the things I saw today," I said. "See you Monday!"

3

Thirteen Little Dishes

"I hope you like Korean food," Mee-Yung's father, Dr. Kim, said as she introduced me to him. "Usually we eat American food all week and eat Korean food on weekends."

"Do you like American food better?" I asked, turning to Mee-Yung.

"No, it's just that Korean food takes a long time to fix. My mother doesn't have time when she gets home from the bank. It also makes you smell like garlic."

"You mean it makes you smell exotic!" her father said with a laugh.

We went into the dining room. Mee-Yung's parents sat down and then we did.

There was a bowl of soup, a soup spoon, and silver chopsticks by each place. The handles of the spoons and the chopsticks were decorated with a tiny pattern of orange and blue flowers.

We waited for Dr. Kim to pick up his spoon before we began to eat the soup.

Mee-Yung said, "There's bean paste and seaweed in the soup. The little white cubes are *tofu,* made from soybeans."

An older boy came in and sat at the table. "Sorry to be late," he said to Dr. Kim. "My tennis match was tied and we had to play extra games."

"Bonnie," Mee-Yung said, "this is my brother, Peter. He's on the high school tennis team."

"Hi, Bonnie," Peter said.

When we had finished our soup, Alina and Mee-Yung cleared away the soup bowls. Dr. Kim looked at me with a smile. "Would you rather use a fork or will you try the chopsticks?" he asked.

"I'd like to try to eat with these pretty chopsticks."

Mrs. Chung smiled. "Chopsticks are much easier for us."

Alina brought in a big tray filled with dishes. I counted thirteen! The only food I recognized was bean sprouts. Then Alina brought each of us a bowl of rice. On a platter there were whole leaves of lettuce. I thought it might be the salad.

Mrs. Chung picked up a lettuce leaf and said, "Watch me, Bonnie, so you'll know how to make a Korean-style sandwich." She held the lettuce on the palm of her hand. She used chopsticks to pick up a large piece of meat. She put it on the lettuce. Then she added food from some of the small dishes. She folded the

lettuce in from the sides and top and bottom until she had a package of meat wrapped in lettuce.

Mrs. Chung handed the food to me. She held her hand around mine and guided my hand to my mouth. I felt like a baby being fed. When I tasted it, I didn't mind being fed. The food was so good!

"Now try some of the other dishes," Alina said.

"Are they hot?" I asked.

"No, you add sauces to make the food spicy," Mee-Yung said. "You tried a really hot one at the festival. With all our meals we eat a dish called *kimchi* that can be made hot or mild." She pointed to one of the thirteen dishes. "That one is my mother's special hot *kimchi.*"

"My favorite," Dr. Kim said.

Mee-Yung made a face. Then she passed a different dish to me. "Try this *kimchi* instead. It's my favorite, and it won't burn your mouth. We buy it at the grocery store."

"What's in it?" I asked.

"Mostly Chinese cabbage, and sometimes radishes and cucumbers. We add spicy things like garlic, ginger, and red peppers," Mrs. Chung said.

Dr. Kim said, "In old times in Korea, women used to make all their *kimchi.* It was a way of keeping cabbage over the winter and giving people vitamin C. Of course they didn't know about vitamins. They just said it kept you healthy. My mother used to make enough for months. She stored it in a big clay jar called a *tok.*"

"I buy all our kimchi except Dr. Kim's favorite. I make that one when I have time," said Mrs. Chung. "We have kimchi and rice with all our meals."

I looked at the small bowls. "There are so many different dishes!"

"We like lots of vegetables," Mrs. Chung said. She pointed to several dishes. "That's squash, dried seaweed, bean sprouts, and eggplant. The barbecued beef you had in the sandwich is called *pulgogi*."

I made another lettuce sandwich by picking up food from the small dishes with my chopsticks while everyone watched. I didn't spill anything and I didn't take any of the hot *kimchi*.

After dinner, Dr. Kim said, "It's time for a concert. Let's go into the living room."

Alina brought out an instrument I had never seen before. It looked like a board with strings stretched along it. She handed it to her father. "This is an ancient Korean harp called a *komungo*," he said as he began to strum. "Long ago, a court musician was playing one of his compositions on a harp like this one. He looked up and saw a black crane dancing to his music. After that, this was called the Black Crane Harp."

Dr. Kim played for a short while. Then he said to Alina and Peter, "Get your flute and violin."

Mee-Yung sat down at the piano. The four of them played some beautiful music, and when they finished, I clapped.

Dr. Kim smiled. "Music has always been important to Korean people. There are ancient stories about flutes, too. A special flute, when played by the king, could calm the waves on the ocean."

I wanted to hear more music and stories, but it was getting dark and I said it was time for me to go home. "I don't want you walking home alone after dark," Dr. Kim said. "Peter will drive you home."

Peter hadn't talked much during dinner, so I didn't know what to say to him as we rode. I asked, "How's school?"

"It's hard," he said. "My father expects so much of me. All I do is play tennis and study."

"Don't you get tired of studying so much?" I thought about how I felt after an hour of doing homework.

"I like to study, but if I don't get all A's I feel I've let my father down."

"Why do you have to get all A's?"

"I've got to get into a good university or my parents will be embarrassed. I went to a Korean-American camp last summer. The kids there talked about how hard it was to take so much pressure. But we all want to make our parents proud, so we try our best. It's not just for my father. It's for the family's honor."

"Can't you talk to your father about how you feel?" I asked.

"I know he'd say it's the Korean way, and he'd tell me about Confucian principles."

"What are they?"

"*Confucius* was a great teacher who lived long ago. He thought the world would be better if all people followed his principles or rules."

19

"Are they like classroom rules?"

"Much more than those," said Peter. "They're about how people should treat each other. Like treating older people and authorities with respect. And obeying your parents. That's why I try to please my father."

"That sounds like what I learn in Sunday school," I said.

"A lot of the ideas are the same. Confucius said that education is important. So my father would end his talk by telling me to study harder."

We'd reached my house. "Thanks for taking me home, and good luck in school, Peter," I said.

4

Special Celebrations

On Tuesday in social studies we had report planning time.

"Did you get your pictures developed?" Mee-Yung asked.

"Yes, here they are." I put the prints on the table.

"They're great! Here's me and Alina on the float, and Chi-Won in the parade, and *Hodori,* the Olympic tiger, and . . ." She turned to see Chi-Won looking over her shoulder.

"How are you doing, Chi-Won?" I asked.

"I lost my partner because he moved." Chi-Won looked sad.

Mee-Yung and I looked at each other. "Would you like to work with us?" we both asked.

Chi-Won smiled. "That would be great!"

We told him what we had done so far. "What Korean-American customs can you add to these?" I asked.

"I could tell about my little brother's first birthday party," he said.

"What's special about that?" I asked.

"It's a big celebration and we found out about my brother's future," Chi-Won said.

"How did you do that?"

"My father put a book, a spool of thread, and some money in front of my little brother. We all watched while he picked up the one he wanted. Everyone was happy when he took the book because that meant he'd be a good student."

"The thread stands for a long life, and the money stands for being rich," Mee-Yung said.

"You were glad he picked being a student instead of having a long life or being rich?" I asked.

Chi-Won said, "My parents think it's better to be a good student. My father said he came to this country so my three brothers and I could get a good education."

"Peter told me about education and Confucius," I said.

"It's important to everyone," Chi-Won said. "My father's going to school, too. He's studying English."

"Can you bring some pictures of your brother for our report?" I asked.

"I can bring my little brother himself, dressed in the Korean clothes he wore for his birthday," Chi-Won said.

"Terrific!" I said. Then I asked Chi-Won and Mee-Yung, "What do you do for other birthdays?"

"Just what you do," said Chi-Won. "Except for the *hwan-gap* celebration on people's sixtieth birthdays.

We celebrated my grandfather's before he died last year. All my relatives went to his house. Everyone bowed to him to show their respect."

"In our family, we do that on New Year's Day," Mee-Yung said. "We bow to our parents and grandparents."

Chi-Won said, "We celebrate on New Year's Day, too. It was the same kind of ceremony on my grandfather's *hwan-gap*. But he was the only one we honored that day."

They were talking about things I didn't understand. I reminded Mee-Yung that she had promised to tell me about Korean New Year's Day.

"You'd like it, Bonnie," Mee-Yung said. "Everyone wears *hanbok*. I like the black hats the older men wear. They're called *kat*, and they look like small top hats with wide brims. And everyone plays games."

"Wait a minute, Mee-Yung," Chi-Won interrupted. "You've left a lot out."

"Okay. First, we get up very early. When everyone is dressed we have a ceremony for our ancestors."

"We call them 'Honored Dead,'" said Chi-Won.

Mee-Yung nodded. "And part of the ceremony in our family is for my father's parents. They're buried in Korea. My father writes their names on paper. He stands the paper next to the wall on a small table. Each of us bows before the paper to show our respect."

"Show me how you do it," I said.

Mee-Yung got on her knees and slowly bowed forward until her head touched the floor.

"Let me try that." I got down on my knees and bowed, but I felt clumsy.

Mee-Yung said, "Bonnie, you need more practice."

Chi-Won went on explaining. "After our family's ceremony, we go to my uncle's house because he's the oldest son."

"We go to my grandparents' house," Mee-Yung said. "We have another family bowing ceremony."

"You sure do a lot of bowing!"

Mee-Yung went on. "About nine o'clock in the morning we have a huge meal with all kinds of good food. We always have rice cakes. Some of my aunts cook for three days for the celebration. After eating, we play games, especially *Yut.*"

"That's a board game like Parchesi or Sorry. We use special sticks instead of dice. I can bring my *Yut* board to school," Chi-Won said.

When he said "board" I remembered the board the boys broke in the parade. I asked Chi-Won to tell me more about *Tae Kwon Do.*

The bell rang. "If you want to come to my house after school, I'll tell you more and show you some things," he said.

Mee-Yung and I said we'd be there.

"I guess I should tell you that my mother doesn't speak English," Chi-Won said.

"I can talk with her," Mee-Yung said. "I've been studying Korean for four years, and we speak Korean at home most of the time."

5

School on Saturdays

That afternoon we went to Chi-Won's house. When he introduced us to his mother, she smiled and bowed her head a little. Mee-Yung and I bowed our heads, too.

Chi-Won brought out his *Tae Kwon Do* uniform and some cloth belts. He handed me a white belt. "This was my first one," he said. "When I learned all the moves and kicks for the first level, I passed a test. I moved to a yellow, then an orange, then purple, and now I am a green belt." He held out each colored belt as he named it. "There are ten levels and the black belt is the highest. I have five more levels to go before I can be a black belt."

"Is *Tae Kwon Do* just the Korean name for karate?" I asked.

Chi-Won shook his head. "They're both martial arts, but *Tae Kwon Do* uses kicking more than karate does and it's much older than karate. It's taught all over

the world. My teacher, Master Huh, says it was intro-duced as an exhibition game at the 1988 Seoul Olym-pics. Now it'll be a regular Olympic event."

Chi-Won's mother and Mee-Yung began talking. "She says that Chi-Won will demonstrate some moves for you, if you'd like," Mee-Yung said.

"Oh, yes!" I agreed.

Chi-Won went to put on his *Tae Kwon Do* uniform while Mee-Yung and Chi-Won's mother talked.

"She's very proud of Chi-Won," Mee-Yung said.

When Chi-Won came back he said, "I'll show you some kicks."

He swung his foot so high that it was way above his head. Then he spun around and kicked with his other foot.

"Wow! That looks hard!" I said.

"It takes a lot of practice!" he told me.

Mee-Yung and I said goodby to his mother. On the way home Mee-Yung asked, "Do you want to come to Korean school with me on Saturday? That's where Chi-Won learns *Tae Kwon Do,* and there's lots more to see there."

"I'd love to," I said, "Where is it?"

"It meets at the junior high. Come by my house and we'll go with Alina and Peter."

At the Korean school I met the principal, Mr. Park. Mee-Yung explained about our report. Mr. Park said, "It's good to learn about each other's customs. During the week our students learn American ways and on Saturdays they learn Korean ways."

"May I take Bonnie around to see the classes?"

"Yes, we'd be happy to have her visit." As he walked with us, he explained, "Our students come for three hours. They learn the history of Korea and to read and write our Korean language. We also have classes in art, music, and *Tae Kwon Do*." He suggested that Mee-Yung take me to the young children's class first.

We went into a classroom where little children were quietly drawing Korean letters. Mee-Yung introduced me to the teacher.

"Would you like to learn some *Hangul*, the Korean alphabet?" the teacher asked. When I nodded, she handed me a work sheet with symbols on it. "Just copy these," she said.

I looked at the small children copying their work sheets. I thought that if they could do it, I'd have to try. I worked hard and finished the paper.

Mee-Yung said, "Let's go see the drum class."

We went to the multipurpose room. I heard the drums before we got there. To my surprise Peter was teaching the class. He asked the drummers to demonstrate some rhythms.

Then Peter asked one of the drummers to tell us about the drums. "They're called *changgo* drums," the boy said. "In Korea there were farmers' bands that played the drums while the farmers worked. Now they're played at celebrations and parades."

"I saw those drums at the Harvest Festival," I said.

Next we went to the *Tae Kwon Do* class and saw Chi-Won. One of the boys laughed and waved to us.

The instructor frowned at him and called his name in a harsh voice. He pointed at the wall. The boy looked embarrassed and went to sit by the wall.

"That's Master Huh," Mee-Yung said.

"Attention!" Master Huh yelled, and the boys and girls in the class stood straight and stiff. "You need strong minds to do *Tae Kwon Do*," he said. "You need to pay attention and concentrate."

"What a strict teacher!" I said to Mee-Yung.

We turned to leave and I saw Mr. Park standing behind us. I knew he had heard what I said. I hoped it hadn't made him angry.

He looked at me and said, "Master Huh may seem strict to you, Bonnie, but we teach respect for teachers, parents, and leaders. That makes all of us better students and better people." He smiled and I knew he wasn't angry with me.

"Thank you for letting me visit."

"Come back again," he said as he walked toward his office.

6

The Korean-American Team

In social studies, each report team met to make plans.

"Let's make a list of things to talk about and show," Mee-Yung said.

It was a long list. We began with things from the festival parade—the Korean clothes and the drums. From Mee-Yung's house we added the perfume case and the picture of the celadon vase.

"And the Korean food and the chopsticks," I reminded Mee-Yung.

"And special birthdays," Chi-Won added.

"What else?" I asked.

"We could show the *Hangul* alphabet," Chi-Won said. "And tell about how it was invented."

I asked him to tell me.

"*Hangul* was invented about the time Columbus discovered America," Chi-Won said. "King Sejong had his court scholars work on it for several years."

"Couldn't Koreans write before that?" I asked.

"Sure," Chi-Won said, "but until *Hangul* was invented, Korean people wrote in Chinese. And that's hard. Chinese symbols stand for words and you have to learn about twenty thousand of them in order to write. *Hangul* is a lot easier to learn. It has twenty-four letters that stand for sounds. We make words out of the letters."

"We could show the class how to write *Hangul*," Mee-Yung said. "Bonnie could do that. She learned some *Hangul* last Saturday."

I knew Mee-Yung was teasing and I shook my head. "I need more lessons before I can do that," I said.

Chi-Won said, "I'll draw some letters and I'll bring some newspapers like *The Korea Times* and *The Dong A Daily News* so the kids in class can see printed *Hangul*."

Mr. Clark called for our attention and made a surprise announcement. "There will be an award for the best report. I didn't tell you sooner because I wanted you to think more about cooperating than competing. Everyone will vote on which report is best."

7

Presenting Korean-American Ways

We drew numbers to see in what order the reports would be given. We were last!

"No one is going to listen to us. They'll be tired of reports by the time we give ours," I complained.

Mee-Yung said, "We need something really special to get their attention. Chi-Won, could you do some *Tae Kwon Do?*"

"Sure. Don't worry. Our report will be great."

I wanted to believe him, but I was still worried.

The reports started on Monday. Ours was scheduled for Wednesday after recess. Some of the reports were good, especially those that included samples of food. Others were just plain BORING.

Tuesday was bad news day. Chi-Won told us he would have to miss part of school on Wednesday. He had forgotten that it was the anniversary of his grandfa-

ther's death. He had to go to his uncle's house for the ceremony.

"I might not get back in time for the report," he said, "but I have to go."

Mee-Yung and I looked at each other. That meant his little brother couldn't be there either. "There goes our report," I said. "Without your part, Chi-Won, we won't win."

"I'm really sorry. I hope I can make it on time."

On Wednesday, Mee-Yung and I watched the clock. There was no sign of Chi-Won. "How long does their ceremony take?" I asked.

"I'm not sure," Mee-Yung said. "There's a meal and then speeches. Chi-Won has lots of relatives, so the speeches could take a long time."

During recess we arranged the chairs in a circle. Then we changed into *hanbok*. We'd just have to give the report without Chi-Won.

The kids came in from recess. Mee-Yung and I stood together and announced, "PRESENTING KOREAN-AMERICAN WAYS!"

We took turns talking. Mee-Yung showed the perfume case and the picture of the celadon vase while she told about them. She talked about Korean food and showed some *kimchi*. I held up Chi-Won's drawings of the Korean letters and told the story of *Hangul*. We passed around the pictures I took at the parade. Mee-Yung let some kids beat the *changgo* drum.

Dr. Kim, who had taken time from his office, showed

the class the Black Crane Harp, played it, and told its story.

We had moved out of the circle and were bowing to the class when suddenly there was a loud shout of "Hiyuh!" The door opened. Chi-Won and three boys from the *Tae Kwon Do* class ran into the classroom. They quickly got into the formation they had used in the parade. One boy held a square board above his head. Another boy ran to Chi-Won's back, then jumped to the third boy's shoulders. He leaped, and with a shout, kicked the board and broke it. Mee-Yung and I were surprised and so was everyone else. All the kids stood up and cheered.

Pinned to the bulletin board was an envelope for each report. Mr. Clark gave everyone in the class a popsicle stick. "Put your stick in the envelope of the report you liked the best," he said.

The voting was finished. I looked at the envelopes. The one marked "KOREAN-AMERICAN WAYS" had the most sticks.

"You're the winners! Your report was good because you had so many things to show as you talked," Mr. Clark said. He handed us certificates that said "SALAD BOWL PROJECT: FIRST PLACE."

"I'm so glad we won," Mee-Yung said when school was over.

"Me, too," I said as I hugged her. "But I won more than first place for a report. I won a best friend!"

Glossary

celadon famous Korean pottery with a special glaze.

changgo hourglass-shaped drum.

chima the skirt of Korean clothing.

chogori the blouse of Korean clothing.

Confucius a Chinese philosopher and teacher who lived about 2500 years ago.

hanbok Korean clothing.

Hangul the Korean alphabet.

Hodori the Korean tiger mascot for the 1988 Seoul Olympics.

hwan-gap a party for the sixtieth birthday.

kat a traditional Korean man's hat.

kimchi a dish made from Chinese cabbage, other vegetables, and spices.

komungo an ancient Korean harp, also called the Black Crane Harp.

Korean New Year's Day celebrated on the first day of the first new moon of the year.

Kugak a Korean association that preserves the traditional music and dances of Korea.

perfume case a tasseled ornament worn on a *hanbok* or used as a wall decoration.

pulgogi strips of barbecued beef.

Tae Kwon Do Korean martial art.

tofu a food made from soybeans.

tok a jar used for storing kimchi.

yut a Korean game.

Some Books about Korea

Farley, Carol. *Korea, A Land Divided.* Minneapolis: Dillon Press, 1983

Kubota, Makoto. *South Korea.* Milwaukee: Gareth Stevens Publishing, 1987

Lye, Keith. *Take a Trip to South Korea.* New York: Franklin Watts, 1985

McNair, Sylvia. *Korea.* Chicago: Childrens Press, 1986

Patterson, Wayne and Hyung-Chan Kim. *The Koreans in America.* Minneapolis: Lerner Publications Co., 1977

Sobol, Harriet. *We Don't Look Like Our Mom and Dad.* New York: Coward-McCann, Inc., 1984

About the Authors

Dianne MacMillan grew up in St. Louis, Missouri, and graduated from Miami University in Ohio with a Bachelor of Science Degree in Education. She taught school for many years but now spends her time writing. Her stories have appeared in *Highlights for Children, Jack and Jill,* and *Cobblestone,* and she is the co-author of *My Best Friend, Martha Rodriguez* and *My Best Friend, Duc Tran.* She lives in Anaheim, California, with her husband and three children.

Dorothy Rhodes Freeman is an educator and author of twenty-one books, including *Someone for Maria* and *A Home for Memo.* She is also the co-author of *My Best Friend, Martha Rodriguez* and *My Best Friend, Duc Tran.* Mrs. Freeman currently writes bilingual education projects and monitors and evaluates the results. Writing is both her vocation and hobby. She has two grown children and lives with her husband in Placentia, California.